Peedie

Olivier Dunrea

HOUGHTON MIFFLIN HARCOURT
Boston   New York

WWW.HMHBOOKS.COM/FREEDOWNLOADS
ACCESS CODE: CAP

AGES	GRADES	GUIDED READING LEVEL	READING RECOVERY LEVEL	LEXILE® LEVEL
4–6	I	F	9–10	300L

www.hmhco.com

The text of this book is set in Shannon.
The illustrations are ink and watercolor on paper.

The Library of Congress Cataloging-in-Publication Data is on file.

ISBN: 978-0-618-35652-2 hardcover
ISBN: 978-0-618-75506-6 board book
ISBN: 978-0-544-32355-1 paper over board reader
ISBN: 978-0-544-32356-8 paperback reader

Manufactured in China
SCP 10 9 8 7 6 5 4 3 2 1
4500499896

For Lily and Bobby

This is Peedie.

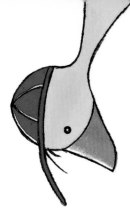

Peedie is a gosling.

A small, yellow gosling
who sometimes forgets things.

Peedie forgets things.
Even when Mama Goose
reminds him.

He forgets to come in
out of the rain.

He forgets to eat all his food.

He forgets to tidy his nest.

He forgets to take a nap.

He forgets to turn the egg.

But Peedie never forgets to
wear his lucky baseball cap.

He wears it everywhere
he goes.

He wears it when he dives.

He wears it when he slides.

He wears it when he explores.

He wears it when he snores.

Peedie never forgets to wear
his lucky red baseball cap.

Everywhere he goes.

Then one day Peedie put
his lucky red baseball cap in
a secret place.

But he forgot where he put it.

He looked in the pond.

He looked in the apples.

He looked under the
flower pot.

He looked in the tall grass.

But Peedie could not
remember where he
had put it.

"Did you forget to turn the egg?" Mama Goose asked.

Peedie slowly trudged to the nest. His lucky red baseball cap was gone.

Then he saw it.
"There you are!" he said.

Peedie is a gosling.
A small, yellow gosling
who forgets things—
sometimes!